A TOAD FOR TUESDAY

A TOAD
FOR
TUESDAY

RUSSELL E. ERICKSON

pictures by
LAWRENCE DI FIORI

Lothrop, Lee & Shepard Co. / New York

10

Library of Congress Cataloging in Publication Data

Erickson, Russell E
  A toad for Tuesday.

SUMMARY: On Thursday a toad is captured by an owl who saves him
to eat on Tuesday, the owl's birthday, but the intervening five days change
his mind.
  [1. Friendship—Fiction] I. Di Fiori, Lawrence, illus. II. Title.
PZ10.3.E68To   [Fic]   73-19900
ISBN 0-688-41569-5
ISBN 0-688-51569-X (lib.bdg.)

Books by Russell E. Erickson

The Snow of Ohreeganu
A Toad for Tuesday

A TOAD FOR TUESDAY

On a windy, wintry night, as countless stars were shining bright, deep in the ground, far under the snow, two little toads were having an argument. The two toads lived by themselves in their cozy home. Warton did the cleaning, and Morton did the cooking. Both did their jobs well, and it was, in fact, Morton's marvelous cooking that had started the argument.

After finishing a huge supper they settled back to enjoy dessert. As Morton poured a cup of clover-blossom tea Warton said, "This is the finest beetle brittle I have ever eaten."

"Thank you," Morton replied.

Then Warton said, "I'll bet dear old Aunt Toolia would surely love some."

9

"She certainly would," agreed Morton.

Warton said, "I'm going to put some in a box and take it to her this week."

At that, Morton spilled his hot tea all over himself and jumped so high he bounced off the ceiling. "Why, that's the most ridiculous idea I've ever heard!" he sputtered.

"Why?" said Warton.

"Because," said Morton, "it is winter up there." He pointed towards the crack in the ceiling he had just made, "And it is cold up there, and there is snow up there, but there is one thing you will not find up there—and that's another toad."

When he saw how long Warton's face had grown he was sorry he had spoken so harshly. "Warton," he said, "it's very kind of you to think of it, and it would be a fine idea except for two things. First, you would freeze and second, you would not be able to hop through all that deep snow."

Warton sighed, clasped his fingers and

leaned far back. Morton could see that he was beginning to think. Whenever Warton thought about something he blinked his eyes—one at a time. They began to blink now, slowly at first, then faster, and then faster, and even faster, until suddenly a big grin appeared on his face. "I know how I shall do it," he cried.

"And how is that?" asked Morton.

"Well, so that I don't freeze, I'll wear four of my heaviest coats, three of my most tightly-knit sweaters, two pair of my thickest mittens and my warm cap with the ear flaps. And to go through the snow . . . I'll make some skis."

"Skis? What are skis?" said Morton.

"Something a traveling rabbit told me about last summer, and I know just how to make them."

Morton's jaw dropped open, but he didn't say a word. He knew that once Warton's mind was made up there was no changing it.

For the next three days Warton worked very hard. He made his skis from strong oak tree roots. When he was done they were as handsome a pair of skis as anyone could want. They were sturdy and straight and polished to such a smoothness they felt like silk. He had also made ski poles to push with from porcupine quills and salamander leather.

On Wednesday morning he was ready to leave for Aunt Toolia's. It took quite a while to bundle up in all his warm clothes. The last thing he put on was a little pack Morton had made for him. In it were several lunches, for it would be at least three or four days' travel to Aunt Toolia's home. There were also a few other things which Warton thought he might need, such as an extra pair of mittens and furry slippers. And on the bottom was the box of beetle brittle for Aunt Toolia.

He said goodbye to his brother who was already washing the breakfast dishes.

"Goodbye," said Morton, "and be very, very careful."

Warton started up through the long tunnel that led to the top of the old stump they lived under. When he stepped out he was dazzled. The brilliant snow glistened and glittered, and the deep blue sky was filled with puffy white clouds that drifted over the tall evergreens. Snowbirds twittered gaily as they hopped from branch to branch.

"This is positively beautiful," thought Warton. "But I must be going. It's a long way to Aunt Toolia's, and I'm curious to try my new skis."

He reached down and strapped them on and then gave a strong push. Immediately, the

skis became tangled, sending him tumbling
into a hill of snow. He hopped up quickly
and tried again. This time he went much far-
ther, until he ran straight into a squirrel who
was digging in the snow. Once again he
hopped up, and after apologizing, off he went
again.

Now he was going along quite well. The
more he skied the more he enjoyed it. All
bundled up in his four coats, three sweaters,
two pairs of mittens, and his cap with the
ear flaps, the little toad looked like a tiny ball
skimming over the woodland snow.

14

After he had gone quite a way and when the sun was directly overhead he decided to have some lunch. He saw a perfect place to eat—a large, flat stump sticking out of the snow.

Stepping out of his skis and giving a big jump, he landed on top. He brought out one of his lunches and poured some hot acorn tea. He ate two sandwiches and was just about to bite into a slice of mosquito pie when he heard a strange sound.

It sounded very much like a far-off hiccup. Warton looked around, but he saw nothing. He started to take another bite and again he heard it. This time it seemed to come from below the stump. He hopped over to the edge and cautiously peeked down.

There, sticking out of the snow, were two furry brown legs with tiny white feet and little toes that wiggled and jiggled every time the hiccup was heard. Warton hopped down and began clearing away the snow as fast as he

15

could. When he was done he found that he had uncovered a brown and white furred deer-mouse. His big dark mouse eyes were filled with gratitude.

"Oh, thank you," the mouse said with relief. "That was . . . hic . . . most uncomfortable. It seems that whenever I become upside down I get the hiccups. I was afraid I would remain that way till the snow melts in the spring."

"How did you manage to get stuck upside down?" asked Warton with a blink.

"I was on top of the . . . hic . . . stump having a little snooze in the noon sun as I often do. But this time . . . hic . . . I had a dream that I was a merry-go-round, and before I could wake up I rolled right off the edge of the stump."

16

"I think I have just the thing for you," Warton said, "if you'll hop back up with me."

When they did, Warton gave the mouse some hot tea and right away the hiccups disappeared.

"Thank you again," said the mouse. "That's much better."

"You're very welcome," said Warton. "Do you live near here, by the way?"

"As near as can be," said the mouse. "I live in this stump. And if I may ask, what is a toad like you doing out in the winter time?"

Warton told him about the beetle brittle for Aunt Toolia and how he was traveling on skis. The mouse thought it was a fine idea, but when Warton pointed in the direction in which he was going the mouse's eyes opened wide in dismay.

"Oh, you mustn't go through the wooded valley!" he cried.

"Why?" asked Warton with a blink.

The mouse leaned closer. "Because there is

a certain owl who lives there," he said in a whisper. "Of all the owls in the world, I am sure that that one is the meanest and nastiest of them all. He is so sneaky that he hunts in the daytime when other owls sleep."

"But," said Warton, "I'll have to go through that valley, for if I go any other way I'll surely get lost. But don't worry," he said with a confident smile, "with my new skis I'll dash through that valley so fast the owl will never catch me."

"Then you wait here a moment," said the mouse, and he scampered down the side of the stump and disappeared into a hole. When he returned he had a round box with him. Out of it he took a small scarf. It was colored a most unusual and pretty red. "If you will wear this, all of my relatives who live along the way will know that you are a friend of mine. And if you should get into trouble they will help you in any way they can."

The toad wrapped the scarf tightly around

his neck, and they bid each other farewell. With a quick push, off he went.

Swiftly he sped down the hillside, on and on, until he entered the dark woods at the edge of the valley. The little toad sailed between the trees, he darted under the bushes, he streaked past the rocks. Like a tiny rocket, he swept along the valley.

Just when he was almost through he noticed a dark shadow on the snow—a shadow that was racing right along beside him.

Nervously he looked up, hoping with all his heart that it wouldn't be what he knew it must be.

But it was. Gliding silently on broad wings, just above his head, the owl peered down at him through enormous yellow eyes. He seemed to float through the air with no effort at all.

The terrified toad could hardly take his eyes away. When he did, it was too late. A wall of old stones was suddenly in front of him. He tried to turn, but there was not enough time. Into the wall he crashed. He popped out of his skis and rolled and tumbled along the wall until he stopped in a heap.

When he brushed the snow from his eyes, the owl was standing on a log staring at him.

"Do I see a toad under all that clothing?" said the owl.

"Yes, you do," said Warton.

"In the middle of winter?"

"I'm going to visit my Aunt Toolia."

"Well, now you are going to visit me . . ." said the owl, "until next Tuesday, that is."

Warton tried to hop away, but one foot hurt so badly he couldn't move. The owl came

20

closer, walking very slowly. Warton closed his eyes. As he did he thought he heard a whisper.

He looked around, only to see that the chill wind was blowing small puffs of snow through holes in the stone wall, and he knew that no one was there at all.

Then strong claws wrapped around him. He heard the soft flapping of wings, and he felt the air of the deep woods grow cold as he was lifted into the sky.

Warton found himself being whisked over the tops of the trees. The evergreens below had the appearance of a thick carpet. The owl traveled fast and silently.

The winter sun was far down when Warton noticed that they were heading towards a particularly large spreading oak. The owl swooped through its snarly branches and into a hole near the top.

It was dark inside and smelled musty. The owl sat the toad in a corner and stepped back. He gave him a piercing look.

"What's your name?" he said.

"Warton."

"Warton?" said the owl. "Well, I think I'll call you . . . Warty."

"I don't care for that very much."

"You don't? Well, that's too bad . . . Warty!"

The little toad got up all his courage and looked right at the owl. "Are . . . are you going to eat me?"

The owl opened his yellow eyes wide. "Am I going to eat you? Of course I'm going to eat you!" Then the owl walked across the room. On the wall a large calendar hung crookedly. The owl pointed at it. "Do you know what this says?"

The toad looked at it closely. "Yes, it says,

BERNIE'S GARAGE
Brakes and Front Ends Our Specialty

"No! I don't mean that. You're not very bright, are you? It says that in five days it will be next Tuesday. And next Tuesday happens to be my birthday. And finding a little toad in the middle of winter is going to make me a special birthday treat. So, until that day, Warty, you may do as you please. From the

looks of your foot I needn't worry about your trying to hop away. Besides, there is no way you can possibly get down from this tree."

The toad looked at his foot. It was twice its normal size. He gave a big sigh. Then he glanced around.

"Tell me, Warty," said the owl, "what do you think of my home?"

Warton looked around again, then he sniffed, then he blinked.

"Well?" said the owl.

"It's terrible," said the toad. "I would certainly hate to live here."

"Don't worry," said the owl, "you aren't going to for long."

"As long as I am here, I would like to make myself comfortable," said Warton. "Do you mind if I light some candles? It seems very dreary in here."

"Dreary?" said the owl. "It seems dreary? Well, go ahead if you want to. It doesn't matter to me."

The toad dug into his pack and pulled out two beeswax candles. As soon as they were lit and began casting their warm glow about the room, he felt much better. He began to straighten his corner. And, being of a cheerful nature, he began to hum a little tune.

The owl couldn't believe his ears. "Warty, you did hear me say that I was going to eat you next Tuesday, didn't you?"

"Yes," said the toad.

The owl shook his head.

Warton continued to busy himself in his corner. Then he turned to the owl and said, "What's your name?"

"I don't know," said the owl. "I guess I don't have one."

"What do your friends call you?"

"I don't have any friends."

"That's too bad," said Warton.

"No, it isn't too bad," snapped the owl. "Because I don't want any friends and I don't need any friends. Now, be quiet!"

Warton nodded. After a while he said, "If you did have a name, what would you like it to be?"

The owl began to be a little flustered. He wasn't used to talking to anyone, especially in his home. "Well, if I had a name . . ." he said slowly, "if I had a name . . . if I had a name . . . I think I would like . . . George."

"Uh huh," said the toad. He went back to straightening his corner.

The owl was becoming sleepy. He fluffed his feathers and closed his eyes.

Just as he was beginning to doze off, the toad called, "Hey, George!"

The owl's eyes popped open. "Are you talking to me?"

27

"Yes," said the toad. "Do you mind if I make some tea?"

"Oh, go ahead," said the flabbergasted owl.

Warton took some more things out of his pack and prepared the tea. While he waited for it to brew he slipped on his furry slippers and wrapped his favorite wooly bathrobe around himself. Shortly, he had a steaming pot of refreshing tea.

"It's ready, George," said the toad.

"What's ready?" growled the sleepy owl.

"Our tea."

"I don't want any."

"But I've already got it poured," said Warton.

"Oh, all right," grumbled the owl.

Then, by the light of the beeswax candles, the owl and the toad sat down to tea.

"May I tell you something?" said Warton.

"What?" said the owl.

"When we were coming here today, even though I was scared as could be, I enjoyed

going through the air like that. It must be wonderful to be able to fly wherever you want to."

"I guess it is," said the owl. Then he thought a bit. "Why yes, it is . . . it's just fine. I'll tell you, Warty, sometimes there's nothing I enjoy more than flying as high as I can and then just drifting along very slowly as I look down on everything. Although, that can be dangerous if you're not careful." He told the toad about a time when he was caught in the dark, rolling clouds of a thunderstorm. And how he was tossed about for hours amid hailstones and crackling streaks of lightning.

Warton was fascinated by the story. "Would you care for another cup of tea, George?"

The owl looked down at his empty cup. "I suppose I might as well," he said.

As Warton poured he said, "That's quite sly of you, George, flying about during the day like that when all other owls are sleeping."

"Is that so!" snorted the owl. "Well, it so happens that I just can't stay awake all night. The last time I tried I fell asleep on my way home, and I flew straight into the biggest beehive I ever saw in my life." The owl shuddered as he remembered that night.

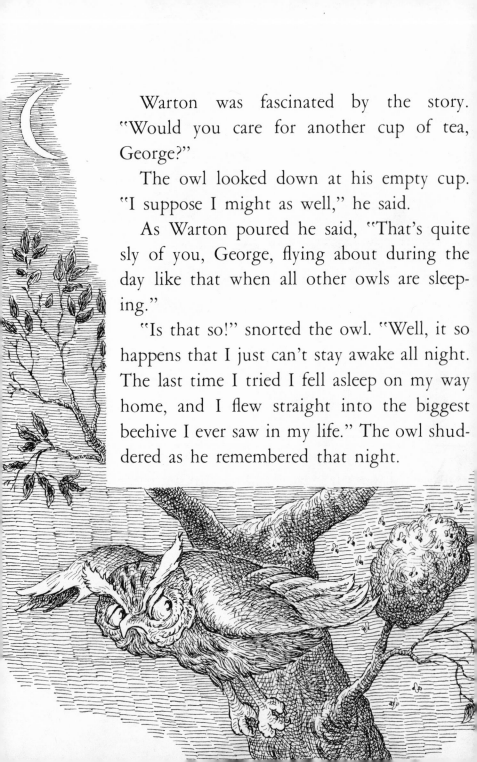

Warton chuckled.

Then the owl talked further and the toad listened. Then the toad talked and the owl listened. It wasn't until the latest hours of that night when the owl finally said, "I'm too tired to talk any more." And he went to sleep.

Warton put away the teacups and then he put out the beeswax candles. As he lay in the still darkness he tried very hard to think of what he should do. But, because of the very busy day he had had and because of all the new experiences, his tired head just would not work at all. He was soon snoring softly.

When the toad awoke the next morning, the owl was gone. The swelling on Warton's foot had gone down but it was still quite sore. The sun shone in through the doorway, and in the bright light of day the owl's home did not seem nearly as gloomy as it had the night before. But it did look every bit as cluttered.

Warton poked through his pack trying to

find something that would be just right for breakfast. He selected an ant-egg salad sandwich. As he unwrapped it his eyes turned to the wall opposite the doorway. A ray of sunlight fell directly on the owl's calendar. A large circle had been drawn around the day of his birthday, and an X put upon the day just past.

Only five days were left!

Warton's appetite nearly vanished, but he managed to eat his breakfast. When he was finished he went to the doorway and looked out.

The snow-covered ground was far, far below, and there was not a branch anywhere near that he could jump to. And even if he did somehow get down from the tree his foot was still too sore to travel on. "I shall just have to wait a bit," he thought.

All this time Warton had been studying the owl's home. Now something was bothering him almost as much as the coming of next

Tuesday. That was the sorry state of the owl's housekeeping. Warton could stand it no longer. Immediately he set about cleaning up the mess.

That was the reason he got along so well with his brother Morton. For, as much as Morton loved to cook, Warton loved to clean up messes. So their home was always neat and sparkling clean. The little toad just couldn't help himself. Before he knew it he was covered with dirt and dust as he hobbled about, being careful not to step too heavily on his sore foot.

All morning and all afternoon he cleaned. He didn't even stop for lunch. He had barely

finished his work when he heard the soft flapping of wings.

The owl had returned a little earlier than usual. He had never thought of cleaning his home himself, so he was astonished at what he saw.

"It doesn't look too bad, Warty," he said. Then he puffed himself up, and his eyes opened wide. "But don't think I'm going to change my mind about next Tuesday."

"I didn't do it for that reason," said Warton. He went to his pack and took out a fresh washcloth. Then he washed off all the dirt and dust that had gotten on him during the day.

When he was done he unwrapped another of the sandwiches Morton had made for him, and quietly ate his supper.

All the while he was eating his sandwich the owl stared straight at him. And all the while he ate his dessert, the owl stared straight at him.

When Warton swallowed the very last bite the owl said, "Are you going to make tea again tonight?"

"Perhaps I will," said Warton.

"Perhaps I will have some too," said the owl softly.

So that night the toad and the owl once again sat down to tea. And once again it was very late before they slept.

The following morning, when the toad awoke, the owl was gone as before. Warton's foot felt much better, so the first thing he did was to look at the calendar. "Only four more days—I must do something soon," he thought anxiously.

He went to the doorway and looked down—it was still just as far to the bottom of the tree. He tried calling to a sparrow, then a chickadee, then a nuthatch, but all the little birds knew the owl lived in that tree. None would come near.

Warton hopped all about, looking for some means of escape. He came upon a few of the owl's last year's feathers that he had somehow missed when he cleaned the owl's home.

"Maybe if I tie some of the feathers to my arms, I could glide to the ground," he thought. Then he laughed aloud at the silliness of the idea.

He decided to clean the owl's home again. When there was nothing left to clean, he ate his lunch. Then he did some jumping exercises to clear his head for serious thinking. When his head was clear, he squatted under the kitchen table and began to think.

First one eye blinked, then the other. Slowly, at first, then faster and faster he blinked, until everything became a blur. Then he stopped, smiling.

He hopped to the doorway again and looked down. "I think two and a half will do it," he said, hopping back to his corner.

Opening his pack, he took out his three tight-ly-knitted sweaters. The blue one, the yellow one, and the white one with the red reindeer.

"There is more than enough strong yarn here to reach the bottom of this tree," he thought.

He began unraveling the blue sweater. And as he unraveled, he tied small loops in the yarn, just far enough apart for him to step into.

"This ladder is going to take me a couple of days," he thought, looking anxiously at the calendar. "And of course, I won't be so warm, and I won't have my skis, but at least I'll be free."

For the rest of the day he unraveled and made loops and hummed softly. When he thought it was almost time for the owl to come home he hid everything in his pack.

It was none too soon, for the owl had returned even earlier than the day before. After supper the two had tea.

Drinking tea always put Warton into a mood for talking. And now that he knew he had a way of escaping he felt relaxed. Over their second cup of tea, he told the owl about the time he and Morton had come home from blueberry picking and found two snakes sleeping on their doorstep. He told how they had tied the snakes' tails together, hit them on their noses with the blueberry pails, then hopped off in different directions. When the snakes tried to catch them they became so snarled that Warton and Morton were able to roll them down the hill like a big ball, straight into the home of a cranky skunk.

The toad chuckled as he told the story.

Then he noticed that the owl was laughing.
"I'm glad you liked the story," said Warton.

"I didn't say that I liked it," snapped the owl.

"But you were laughing," said the toad.

"I was?" said the owl. "I don't believe I ever did that before."

As the toad filled their cups again, the owl said, "This is very good tea."

"Yes, it is," said Warton, "but not as good as my favorite of all teas."

"What is that?" asked the owl.

"Juniper-berry tea. My cousin once brought me some. I've never tasted any as good. But it grows only in certain places and I've never had it again."

And they talked some more.

After Warton blew out the beeswax candles he said, "Goodnight, George."

There was a long, long silence. Then the owl said, "Goodnight, Warty."

The next day was just the same. In the morning when the toad awoke, the owl was gone. Warton worked on his unraveled-sweater-ladder until the owl returned. Later they drank some tea and had a chat.

On Sunday morning, even though his ladder wasn't finished, Warton decided to test it. He fastened one end to the owl's saggy sofa. The other end he dropped out of the doorway. Lying on his belly, he placed one foot over the edge and into the first loop. That one held.

He put his other foot into the next loop. That one held, too. Now he could see all the way to the ground, and it made him dizzy.

But Warton had to be sure that his ladder

would really work. So down he went to another loop, another, and then another. Finally he was satisfied.

Climbing back up was much more difficult. Warton was all out of breath when he crawled into the owl's home. After a few minutes' rest he went back to work on his ladder. From time to time he glanced anxiously at George's clock. Because it had only the small hand it was very difficult to know exactly what time it was.

Finally, even though he had much more to do, Warton dared not work any longer. "Tomorrow I will have to work as fast as I can every possible minute if I am to finish in time," he thought. As he put the ladder in his pack another thought came to him, "Unless . . . unless George changes his mind. Then I won't need this ladder at all." Warton was thinking about how the owl came home earlier and earlier each day and how he seemed to enjoy their chats very much. At times he even seemed almost friendly. "Why, he may not eat me after all!" The thought suddenly made Warton feel quite happy.

But that day the owl returned home later than he had ever done before. It was almost dark when he stepped through the doorway.

Warton was still feeling quite happy. "Good evening, George," he said cheerily. "Did you have a nice day today?"

The owl stood staring down at the toad, his eyes cold as ice. "No . . ." he said slowly, "I did not have a nice day. I have been crunched up in a hollow log since early this morning. I did not catch the mouse that I chased in there, and when I started to come out, a fox was waiting at the entrance. He didn't leave until a short while ago. I have had nothing to eat all day. I am hungry and I am stiff and a storm must be coming because my talons are beginning to ache terribly."

Warton's happiness vanished instantly. He knew now that to depend upon the owl's having a change of heart could be a fatal mistake. The ladder was his only hope, and yet there was so much more work to do and—the toad sighed—so little time.

It was not much later when the wind began howling through the dark woods and fine flakes of snow whipped through the branches of the oak. Indoors it was warm and cozy, and to take his mind off his misery Warton decided to play a game of solitaire. The owl was soaking his talons in a pan of hot water.

As Warton was getting out his deck of cards the owl noticed something else that he took out of his pack.

"What's in that white box, Warty?"

"Beetle brittle," said the toad.

"Perhaps I will have a piece," said the owl.

"Oh, I'm sorry," said Warton, "but this is for my Aunt Toolia."

Because of his aching talons, the owl was already in a bad mood. Now he became angry. "I only want one piece," he snapped. "And besides, what makes you think you are ever going to see your Aunt Toolia again?" He stepped out of the pan and snatched the box away.

Slowly, the owl ate one piece. "Hmmm, this is delicious."

"Of course," said Warton. "Everything my brother makes is delicious."

"Is that so," said the owl. "And I'll just bet your brother would be delicious too."

That made the toad angry.

The owl noticed it. "Oh, I ate only one piece," he grumbled. He closed the box and went to put it away in Warton's pack.

As he did his yellow eyes fell on Warton's ladder.

"Well . . ." he said as he pulled it out of the pack. "Well . . . Well . . . Well. . . ." He walked to the doorway. "Well . . . Well . . . Well . . . Well. . . ." And away went Warton's ladder into the howling wind.

The owl said no more that night.

Warton's heart became heavier than it had ever been in all his life. For the first time, there was absolutely no hope in it.

On the next night, the eve of the owl's birthday, neither one of them spoke at all. The owl just sat, and his great yellow eyes stared straight ahead. The little toad hummed no tune that night. It was still very early when he puffed out the beeswax candles.

For a long, long time he lay awake. He

thought about many things—things he had done and things he had hoped to do. But mostly he thought about his brother. And he knew how much Morton would miss cooking special meals for him. He thought about their tidy home, and wondered if it would become messy. Finally, exhausted by hopelessness and sorrow, he fell into a deep sleep.

As on all the other mornings, when Warton awoke the owl was gone. He washed up as always, but went without breakfast. The day before, he had eaten the last of Morton's lunches.

Sadly he looked at the calendar. There were no more days to be crossed off. This was the owl's birthday.

For a long time Warton sat staring at the calendar. Then, suddenly he heard a sound—a very distant sound. The owl was returning early for his birthday treat, he supposed. What would it be like? Warton wondered with a shudder.

Then he realized that the sound was not coming from outside the tree at all. He listened very carefully. At first it seemed to be coming from one of the dark corners of the room.

He hopped over. Now it seemed to come from within the heart of the tree itself.

Holding his breath, he went on listening. Whatever it was, it was coming closer. Could some other animal live in this tree—an animal that ate toads?

The sound grew louder. Warton could clearly hear the clicking of teeth and the scratching of sharp claws. He looked about for a place to hide, but it was too late.

On the wall, close to the floor, a hole was appearing. Quickly it grew a little larger, then out popped seven or eight delicate whiskers, followed by a tiny nose and furry body. And there, standing before Warton, was a brown and white mouse like the one that had given him the red scarf.

"Hi, I'm Sy," said the mouse, shaking saw-dust from his whiskers.

The toad was overjoyed. "Hello, I'm Warton. I was afraid at first that you were the owl coming home early for his birthday treat, which is me. Then I was afraid that you were some other animal that lived in this tree and liked to eat toads. I've been quite nervous this past day or two."

"I don't blame you," said the mouse, "but don't worry, I and my brothers will help you escape."

"Oh, thank you," said Warton, "but how did you know I was here?"

49

"We were watching you as you traveled through the dark woods. We saw that you were wearing the special scarf. After you crashed into the wall, I whispered to you, but I don't think you heard me."

"I remember a kind of whispering," said Warton. "Was that you? I thought it was the wind."

"That was me all right," said Sy. "When the owl said he was going to take you home and save you for Tuesday, I knew we had a few days to think of a way to help you escape. But I didn't think it would take this long."

"That's all right," said Warton, "I have not been harmed."

"Great!" squeaked Sy, his eyes bright with excitement. "My brothers are waiting for us at the bottom of the tree. So, come! It's time to flee!"

Warton could see that Sy was enjoying the rescue immensely, but he wondered how much protection a few little mice would be.

Quickly, he threw his belongings into the pack. He knew he must leave as soon as possible, yet, when he picked up the beeswax candles he stood for a moment. He could not help but think fondly of the chats he and the owl had had over tea.

"Hurry! Hurry!" ordered Sy in his loudest squeak. "He may return at any moment."

Warton put the candles in the pack along with a scrap of paper that had been lying on the table. He could not leave the owl's home untidy.

Next, he put on every bit of his warm clothing—four coats, one-half of a tightly-knit sweater, two pairs of mittens, and his cap with the ear flaps. Then he followed the mouse into the dark hole.

Beyond it was a narrow passageway, full of twists and turns. Some spots were so narrow the two could just barely squeeze through.

"We're going downward now," Sy said when they reached the center of the old tree. "Hold tightly to my tail or else you'll fall."

Halfway down they passed a small opening. Inside was a family of squirrels just sitting down to breakfast. Warton pictured Morton eating breakfast all alone, and felt homesick.

It was a long way down, but at last they reached the bottom of the giant tree. Blinking in the sunlight, Warton looked around him.

Everything looked beautiful, and the crisp air made him feel good all over.

"Meet my brothers," said Sy proudly.

There, standing on skis exactly like Warton's and leaning on porcupine ski poles, were at least one hundred mice.

"When we saw how fast you traveled on those sticks of yours we decided to make some, too," Sy explained. "Of course, we brought yours along for you."

Warton was speechless. Never had he seen so many mice at one time, and all on skis.

"Let anyone try to stop us now!" shouted Sy. "Right, boys?"

"Right!" squeaked back a hundred voices.

"Then, let's go!" cried Sy.

Forming two long lines, with Warton and Sy in front, off they went. The hundred mice and one toad became a weaving ribbon that wound swiftly through the trees of the wooded valley. As they sped by, the other creatures of the woods stared in astonishment.

Rabbits gawked, squirrels gaped, and birds gasped. No one had ever seen such a sight before.

As they zipped along, Warton said, "I never dreamed you had so many brothers, Sy."

"They're not even all here," said Sy. "Because of the accidents."

"Accidents?" said Warton.

"Yesterday, when we were trying our new skis for the first time, fourteen of my brothers ran into each other," Sy explained. "Seven turned their ankles, four banged their noses, and three backed into ski poles and won't be able to sit down for at least a week."

Then he began to sing a stirring marching song. The two brothers behind him joined in, then the next two, and the next, until the whole, string of skiing mice were singing loudly as they whooshed along.

After they had gone some distance, they came to an open meadow on a hillside. At the bottom was an icy stream.

"We'll rest here a short time," said Sy. "When we're refreshed, we will finish our journey."

"Good," said Warton. "That will give me a chance to thank you and all your brothers—" He never finished, for something had caught his eye.

Down below, near the stream, some kind of a struggle was going on. Puffs of snow flew in every direction. Even from such a distance, a great deal of screeching and growling could be heard. When the snow cleared away for an instant, Warton saw someone he thought he knew.

"George?" he said under his breath. Shading his eyes from the bright sun, he looked again.

He was right. George the owl was struggling frantically to free himself from the jaws of a snarling fox. Warton could see at once that George didn't have the slimmest chance. Even now, the owl's wings were flapping weakly against the snow, while flying feathers filled the air.

Warton hopped to his feet and strapped on his skis.

"Where are you going?" asked Sy.

"I'm going to help George."

"George? Who's George?"

"George, the owl," said Warton.

"But . . . but . . . I thought we were helping you to get away from him," said Sy in bewilderment.

"Yes," said Warton, "but I just can't stand here and watch that fox eat him."

"But, he was going to eat *you*."

Warton wasn't listening. He pushed off toward the icy stream.

Sy scratched his head. "I never did understand toads. Well, come on, my brothers!" he squeaked with a twitch of his whiskers. "Let's give him a hand."

At once, all the mice jumped onto their skis and pushed off after Warton. The sunny hillside was one great wave of skiing mice as they flashed over the glistening snow. A powdery cloud rose high behind them as the one hundred mice and one toad swept downwards.

The fox looked up and blinked unbelievingly. Faster and faster they came, the sharp points of their poles glittering like diamonds and each one pointing straight at him. Quickly the fox decided that he wanted no part of whatever it was.

He released the owl, and bounded off through the deep snow as fast as his shaking legs would go.

The toad was the first to reach the owl. Most of the mice stopped a safe distance away, but Sy and a few of his brothers kept right after the terrified fox.

Warton looked sideways at the crumpled owl. Feathers were scattered all over the snow. Some floated slowly away in the icy stream. The owl's wings were badly tattered and one of his big yellow eyes was swollen completely shut.

As he looked at the once proud bird, Warton felt sad.

"Hello, Warty," said the owl weakly.

"Hello, George," said the toad.

"What are you doing here?" asked the owl.

"I'm escaping."

The owl's one good eye opened wide. "Escaping? Escaping from what?" he said, clearly annoyed.

"From you," said the toad. "Today is your birthday, and you said you were going to eat me. I was to be your special treat."

The owl started to shake his head, but it hurt too much. "Didn't you see my note?" he said, sounding more and more exasperated.

Then Warton remembered the piece of paper he had cleared from the table. "I—I didn't have time."

"Well, if you had, you would have known that I was coming home soon, and that I was going to bring a surprise."

"A surprise?" said Warton.

"That's what I said. I first came here to the stream to get a nice fish for supper, which I did. But, the surprise is over there, and that's where the fox caught me." The owl turned and pointed to some bluish-green bushes.

"Why, those are juniper bushes," said the toad.

"That's right," said the owl. "You said juniper berries made your favorite kind of tea, didn't you?"

Warton hardly knew what to say. "But I don't understand . . . do you mean you came here to pick them for me, and you weren't going to eat me, ever?"

"Of course I was going to eat you—until last night, that is." The owl spoke more softly. "Because we weren't speaking, I thought quite a bit last night. I thought about our chats and other things, and I thought that perhaps having a friend might not be too bad. I mean . . . I don't need any friends, of course . . . but. . . ." As he spoke, two feathers fluttered to his feet. Then the owl turned his head so that Warton couldn't look at him. When he spoke again his voice was so soft the toad could barely hear him. "But if I ever do have a friend . . . I hope he is just like you . . . Warton."

Warton was stunned. From somewhere deep inside, a small lump had come into his throat. "Do you mean you would like us to be friends?" he said.

The owl nodded his head.

Then the toad hopped around to where he could look up at him. "I would be happy to be your friend, George."

The owl looked down and a big smile slowly spread across his battered face. "Well, that's fine. That's just fine. I'm so happy I promise I'll never eat another toad again." He

looked around at Sy and his brothers, "Or a mouse, for that matter."

The mice cheered.

"Now, if I can still fly," he said, shaking out a few more loose feathers, "I'd be glad to take you the rest of the way to your Aunt Toolia's."

The toad hopped onto his back, shouting goodbye and thank you to Sy and to all his brothers. It took the owl some time to lift out of the snow, but finally he rose into the

air. The higher he flew, the stronger he became. Warton waved to the mice as, far below,
they grew smaller and smaller. Then the forest
trees seemed to float beneath them as they
made a great circle in the blue sky and turned
towards Aunt Toolia's.